FIVE LITTLE DUCKS

NorthSouth
New York / London

Five Little Ducks

AN OLD RHYME · ILLUSTRATED BY

Pamela Paparone

Published in the United States by North-South Books Inc., New York 10001.
Published simultaneously in Great Britain, Canada, Australia, and New Zealand in 1995
by North-South Books Inc., an imprint of NordSüd Verlag AG, CH-8005 Zürich, Switzerland.
First paperback edition published in 1997.

Library of Congress Cataloging-in-Publication Data
Paparone, Pamela.
Five little ducks: an old rhyme / illustrated by Pamela Paparone.
Summary: When her five little ducks disappear one by one, Mother Duck sets out to find them.
1. Nursery rhymes. 2. Children's poetry. [1. Nursery rhymes. 2. Ducks—Poetry. 3. Counting.] I. Title.
PZ7.P196Fi 1995 95-13136

A CIP catalogue record for this book is available from The British Library.
The artwork was created with acrylic paint and colored pencil.
Designed by Marc Cheshire
ISBN: 978-1-55858-700-7 (PAPERBACK)
9 PB 10
ISBN: 978-0-7358-1857-6 (BOARD BOOK)
3 5 7 9 BB 10 8 6 4 2
Printed in China by Leo Paper Products Ltd., Heshan, Guangdong, December 2010.

www.northsouth.com

To J.O. with love

Five little ducks went out one day,
Over the hills and far away.

Mother duck said,
"Quack, quack, quack, quack."
But only four little ducks came back.

Four little ducks went out one day,
Over the hills and far away.

Mother duck said,
"Quack, quack, quack, quack."
But only three little ducks came back.

Three little ducks went out one day,
Over the hills and far away.

Mother duck said,

"Quack, quack, quack, quack."

But only two little ducks came back.

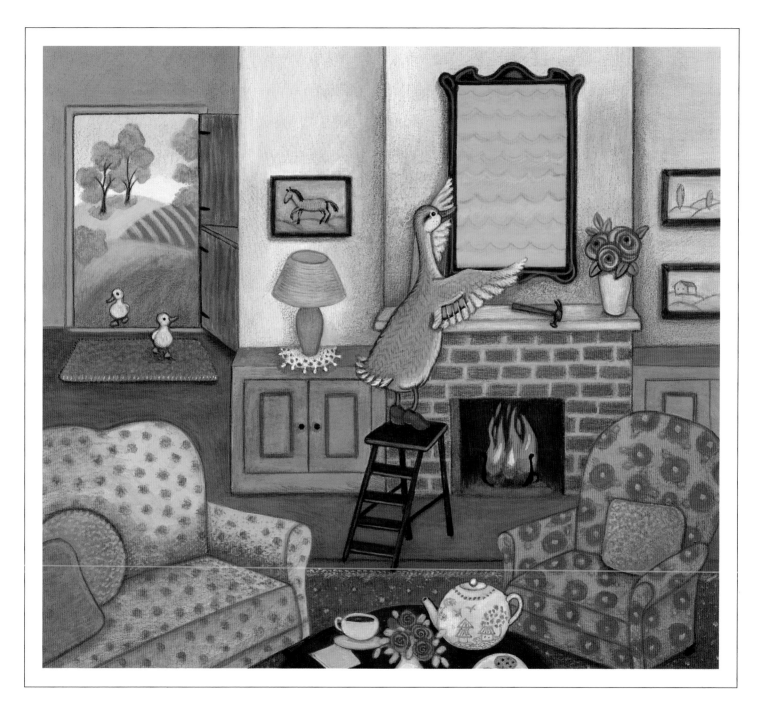

Two little ducks went out one day,
Over the hills and far away.

Mother duck said,
"Quack, quack, quack, quack."
But only one little duck came back.

One little duck went out one day,
Over the hills and far away.

Mother duck said,
"Quack, quack, quack, quack."
But none of the little ducks came back.

Sad mother duck went out one day,
Over the hills and far away.

Mother duck said,
"Quack, quack, quack, quack."

And all of her five little ducks came back!